A little angel grows up

"I have the perfect task for you, little angel," said the Archangel of Independence. "Are you ready to come?"

The little angel had been expecting to be given another task soon. But he didn't like the way the archangel asked that question. "In the past, I've done all my tasks with a little angel partner. Can't I have a partner this time?

"You won't need one." The Archangel of Independence smiled. "This is a task for you—not for any other little angel. But I'll be by your side as long as you need me."

Aladdin

Angelwings

№. 3

On Her Own

On Her Own

Donna Jo Napoli

illustrations by Lauren Klementz-Harte

Aladdin Paperbacks

Thank you to all my family,
Brenda Bowen, Noëlle Paffett-Lugassy, and Richard Tchen

First Aladdin Paperbacks edition November 1999
Text copyright © 1999 by Donna Jo Napoli
Illustrations copyright © 1999 by Lauren Klementz-Harte

Aladdin Paperbacks
An imprint of Simon & Schuster
Children's Publishing Division
1230 Avenue of the Americas
New York, NY 10020

Designed by Steve Scott
The text for this book was set in Minister Light and Cheltenham.
The illustrations were rendered in ink and wash.
Printed and bound in the United States of America
2 4 6 8 10 9 7 5 3 1

Library of Congress Cataloging-in-Publication Data
Napoli, Donna Jo, 1948–
On her own / Donna Jo Napoli ; illustrations by Lauren Klementz-Harte.
— 1st Aladdin Paperbacks ed.
p.   cm. — (Aladdin Angelwings ; #3)
Summary: The Little Angel of Independence helps a girl named Elena
develop independence and self-reliance when she loses her beloved toy
giraffe during a visit to the park.
ISBN 0-689-82985-X (pbk.)
[1. Angels—Fiction. 2. Self-reliance—Fiction. 3. Giraffes—Fiction.
4. Toys—Fiction. 5. Lost and found possessions—Fiction. 6. Parks—Fiction.]
I. Klementz-Harte, Lauren, 1941–   ill. II. Title.
III. Series: Napoli, Donna Jo, 1948–
Aladdin Angelwings ; #3.
PZ7.N150p   1999
[Fic]—dc21   99-27370
CIP

For my Elena

Aladdin

Angelwings

№ 3

On Her Own

Angel Talk

I have the perfect task for you, little angel," said the Archangel of Independence. "Are you ready to come?"

The Little Angel of Independence looked down at the archangel from his perch in the tree house. He had been expecting to be given another task soon. He loved helping children. And he was looking forward to hearing the bell that would ring when he earned his wings. That couldn't be very far off—he almost had all his feathers already. Still, he didn't like the way the archangel asked that question. His chest tightened. "In the past I've done all my tasks with a little angel partner. Can't I have a partner this time?"

"You won't need one. The problem is obvious."

"To you," said the little angel. "But it might not be so obvious to me."

The Archangel of Independence smiled. "This is a task for you—not for any other little angel. But I'll be by your side as long as you need me."

The little angel waved good-bye to his friends and climbed down the ladder. He took the archangel's hand.

Off they went to a schoolroom. The little angel stayed very close to the archangel as he looked around. Both of them were invisible to the children. Still, they held back in a corner, out of the way.

The children sat at their desks coloring the fronts of large manila envelopes. Sweat beads formed across their brows, despite the open windows. One boy stopped for a moment and gazed out at the empty playground. A girl scratched her ankle, then got absorbed in readjusting the straps on her new sandals. Other than that, the class was busy.

"They look pretty normal to me," said the Little Angel of Independence. "No one's nagging the teacher for extra directions or copying a friend's artwork or anything else that shows a weak spirit. How can I tell who's lacking independence?"

The Archangel of Independence stood beside him, attentive and quiet, as though he hadn't heard a word the little angel said.

The little angel yanked on the archangel's hand, which he still held tight. "Whom should I help?"

"Try to figure it out," said the Archangel of Independence.

The teacher rapped his desk with his knuckles. "Okay, everyone. Now take the loose papers from your desks and slide them into your envelopes. I'm going to pass back your last few quizzes for you to put in, too." He got up and walked down the aisles handing back sheets of paper. "Be sure to show them to your parents."

The children obediently lifted their desk lids and stuffed their envelopes. One boy checked to see what his neighbor was doing.

The Little Angel of Independence moved closer to the boy, pulling the archangel with him. "Is it he?"

The boy's hand darted into his neighbor's desk and emerged with a small plastic bag. "These are *my* water balloons. I knew you stole them," he hissed.

The other little boy twisted his mouth to one side. "I was going to give them back. I just forgot."

"Yeah, sure."

"I was. Today, in fact. Since it's the last day of school. I was going to do it today."

The little angel turned away. Stealing was a problem, all right. But that's not the problem he had been chosen to deal with. He looked around the room one more time.

The teacher walked the aisles, holding the trash can. "Put your math books on the back

5

table and your reading books on the shelf by the windows. Then dump anything you want to get rid of into this can."

Two girls got up and hooked arms as they carried their math books to the back table. They looked pretty dependent on each other.

The Little Angel of Independence pulled the archangel with him as he followed the girls.

But then one of them skipped back to her desk, and the other one stayed to neaten up the book stacks as the other children dropped off their math books.

"It's not one of them." The Little Angel of Independence sighed. "Who is it?"

The Archangel of Independence remained silent.

A buzzer went off.

"That's it, kids. The school year is over." The teacher half-sat on the edge of his desk and smiled. "Have a great summer."

Happy conversation broke out all over the room as the children gathered their things and went out the door.

The angels followed them outside.

One little girl with ribbons in her braids had stopped in the middle of the sidewalk to fiddle with her backpack.

"Hey, Elena," called another girl as she passed by, "want to go to the ice-cream store? My mom gave me and my big sister money to celebrate the last day of school."

Elena reached inside her backpack and pulled out a stuffed giraffe. Its matted fur was totally worn off in places, and its neck flopped to one side. "I can't. Kathy doesn't feel like going out, and I've got to take care of her." She kissed the giraffe and tucked it under her arm.

The other girl got on the bus and tapped the shoulder of the girl beside her. She pointed at Elena through the bus window. They both laughed.

Elena slung her backpack over one shoulder and ran for home.

"That's the one I'm supposed to help?" asked the little angel.

The Archangel of Independence nodded. "I knew you'd discover her on your own."

The Lilac Bush

Saturday morning Elena sat at the kitchen table and poured syrup over her pancakes. "Why, Ma? Why can't I come with you?"

Ma put her hands on her hips. "Elena, I told you. I have a zillion errands to run. A kazillion. It wouldn't be any fun for you."

Elena stuffed her mouth with pancakes. "What am I supposed to do, then?" she garbled.

"Sam will take you with him."

"What?" Sam stabbed a second pile of pancakes with his fork and put them on his plate. "I've got a soccer game."

"Elena likes soccer." Ma put the frying pan in the sink and scrubbed.

"Are you crazy? She can't play."

"Just take her with you, Sam."

"She's a girl."

"You know I hate that kind of boy-girl separation. She's got legs. She can play."

"I'm on a *team,* Ma."

Ma dried her hands on the dish towel and grabbed her purse. "I've got to go."

"Don't expect me to—"

"There's plenty of stuff for lunch in the fridge," said Ma, talking fast and loud. "And I'll bring home something nice for dinner."

"Maaaa."

Ma kissed Elena on the cheek. "Be good, baby." She went to kiss Sam, but he ducked. Ma laughed and left.

Sam looked at Elena.

Elena licked the syrup off her plate and carried it to the sink. "Kathy and I will be ready in a minute."

"No way you're bringing that ugly giraffe."

Elena washed her plate. "She goes everywhere with me."

"Well, she doesn't go everywhere with *me.* Either that, or you stay home."

"I'd rather stay home with Kathy, anyway. She's more fun than you."

"You can't really stay home alone and you know it. Ma would freak out." Sam brought his dish over to the sink. "Wash it."

"No fair."

"If I have to be seen with you and that giraffe, you have to wash my dish."

"Oh!" Elena lurched forward over the sink.

"What happened?"

"You know. You shoved me."

Sam made a monster face. "I didn't shove you. I'm way over here. How could I shove you?"

Elena looked over one shoulder, then the other. "If you shove me again, I'll tell Ma when she gets home."

"I didn't shove you. I swear."

"You didn't?" Elena looked around the room. "How weird."

Sam went into the bedroom.

Elena looked around again. She gave a

little shiver. Then she ran the sponge over Sam's dish.

Sam came out dribbling his soccer ball. "Let's go."

Elena dried her hands. She picked up her stuffed giraffe, who had been waiting for her on the chair.

Sam sighed loudly. "Just 'cause Ma babies you all the time doesn't mean you have to act like a baby when she's not here." He went out the apartment door and stood in the corridor. He looked back at Elena meaningfully.

"I have to." Elena clutched Kathy to her chest. "I really have to bring her, Sam."

"That is the most beat-up, revolting stuffed animal in the world. It doesn't even have a tail anymore. And its eyes don't match. One is a button." Sam glowered. "Even a mother couldn't love that face."

"Please, Sam. I washed your dish."

"Don't look at me that way." Sam tossed his soccer ball from hand to hand. "Oh, all right. But walk at least ten feet behind me. No, twenty."

Elena followed Sam, twenty feet behind, down the stairs and out the front door of the building.

When he got to the corner, he stopped and looked over his shoulder.

Elena smiled.

Sam gave a disgusted look and crossed the street. He was walking fast now, tossing his soccer ball as he went.

Elena skipped behind him happily. It didn't matter if she lost sight of Sam, because she knew exactly where he was going. The park was only four blocks away.

Sam waited at the light. He glanced at Elena and motioned for her to catch up.

Elena ran and stood beside Sam.

When the light changed, they crossed together, into the park. They walked the wide, central lane, Elena's favorite path.

A big kid came up beside them on a

skateboard. He gave Sam a short wave.

Sam jerked his chin toward the boy in greeting.

The boy looked at Elena, then rolled his eyes. He zipped off.

Sam turned to Elena. "Why do you have to carry around that piece of junk? Why? Give me one good reason."

"Kathy's my best friend."

Sam blew air through his lips so they made a blubber sound. "Everyone makes fun of you."

"I don't care."

"Everyone makes fun of me because of you."

"Oh." Elena hadn't known people made fun of Sam. Poor Sam. "I'm sorry."

"Then throw her away." Before Elena knew what was happening, Sam grabbed the giraffe and threw it high.

Elena flinched as though she'd been hit.

Kathy caught in the top branches of

a huge, old lilac bush. She looked down at Elena through the clusters of purple blossoms.

"Kathy!" Elena climbed on the bench by the bush and stood on her tiptoes, grabbing frantically over her head, but she still couldn't reach Kathy. She shook the branches. Kathy swung by her neck.

Sam put his hands in his pockets. "Sorry."

"Get her down, Sam." Elena jumped off the bench and pulled hard on Sam's arm. "Get her down now."

"Don't be dumb, Elena. I can't climb that bush. Look how skinny the branches are." Sam dug a hole in the dirt with the tip of his sneaker. "I'm going to my soccer game on the field right over there, okay? Stay in the park and play. Meet me at the jungle gym when the noon church bell rings."

"But what about Kathy?" Elena pulled on her fingers. "Please, Sam. Oh, please."

"I'll bring back a friend. Maybe together

we can get her. I've got to go or I'll be late." Sam ran off.

Elena pressed her hands against her eyes to hold back the tears. Then she looked up at Kathy. "Don't be scared. I'll think of something. I promise."

Angel Talk

"Oh, no." The Little Angel of Independence held on to the archangel's arm. "I shouldn't have shoved her so hard."

"You shoved her? Now I understand. I wondered why she almost fell into the sink."

"A little shove might have given her the confidence to refuse to wash Sam's dish. Then she would have gone to the park without Kathy, strong and independent. But that big shove made her worry, so she needed Kathy. I made a mistake."

The Archangel of Independence cleared his throat. "Little angel?"

The little angel stepped back and looked up at the archangel's face.

"If you hadn't shoved her, she might have insisted on staying home with Kathy. And Sam

20

might have been tempted to leave her alone. That would have been unsafe. You did the right thing. You earned a feather for that shove."

"I did? Wow!" The little angel looked at his wings. The new feather stood out, fluffier than the others. He grinned. But then he remembered the problem. "Only now, Kathy's stuck in that lilac bush. What will Elena do?"

"You heard her. She'll think of something."

"But Sam's right. The branches will break if she tries to climb them. Archangel?"

"What?"

"I weigh nothing; I can climb the bush easily. Then I can knock Kathy off so she falls right into Elena's hands."

"I was afraid you'd think of that. You're always climbing everyplace." The Archangel of Independence leaned over so that his eyes were level with the little angel's eyes. "It doesn't matter how easy it is for you. If you solve Elena's problem, how can she be independent?"

The Little Angel of Independence gulped. "Help me do the right thing for Elena."

"Let's see what Elena thinks of. Then I bet you'll think of something, too."

A Stick

Elena walked up and down the park paths, searching. It seemed the park was filled with short people today. Little kids, of course. But also mothers and baby-sitters who were no taller than Elena's ma, and Elena's ma wasn't tall.

Finally she saw a fairly tall man. She was about to ask him for help, when she stopped short. Ma was always warning about strangers. Even teachers warned. It wasn't a good idea for a little girl to approach a stranger in the park. Elena stood there, silent, watching the man, who leaned against a tree and ate peanuts from a bag. He didn't look dangerous. But, then again, most people didn't.

Okay, so she couldn't ask him for help.

She felt like crying again. She pressed her hands over her eyes.

Oh! Elena looked around fast. Someone had shoved her. "Sam? Was that you? Where are you, Sam?" She ran to the closest tree and peeked behind it. No one. "Sam?"

Elena rubbed her shoulder. Sam couldn't have done it. He was probably racing after a soccer ball—the game had to have started by now. But someone had shoved her. She was sure of it. Yet no one was near. No one.

Well, there was nothing she could do about it. And, anyway, she had an important problem. She had to find someone to get Kathy down from that bush.

Or else she had to do it herself.

How?

A stick. That would work.

Elena walked off the paths now, scanning the ground around the trees and bushes for the perfect stick.

But, wouldn't you know it, there were soda

cans and candy wrappers and old newspapers everywhere, and there were tons of short sticks, but not a single long one.

Elena picked up one short stick. She'd have to be a lot taller for this stick to be of help. She dropped it again. The fact was, Elena couldn't get Kathy without Sam's help. And she couldn't get Sam's help until he finished his soccer game. She might as well give up and cry.

Oh! Elena stumbled from another shove. She spun around. "Who did that?" she called. "Who pushed me?" She put up both fists. "Don't come near or I'll punch you." She jumped to face one side, then the other side, then the rear, like she'd seen boxers do on TV.

A boy in the sandbox stopped playing and looked at Elena, his right hand on a red metal snow-shovel truck that had been plowing a long path around the sand mound. His mother looked at Elena, too.

Elena's cheeks went hot. She walked

quickly past them, out along the main path. Someone was bothering her, that was clear. And that person was fast, whoever it was. Well, Elena could be fast, too.

She ran along the paths.

Someone called out to her, "What's the matter?"

But Elena could hardly make out the words, she was crying so hard.

Angel Talk

T hat's it. We have to talk." The
Archangel of Independence looked
up at the little angel, who sat on the top of the
jungle gym. He shook his head. "Come on
down here."

The little angel jumped and landed right
beside the archangel.

"You're getting carried away with those
shoves."

"They weren't as hard as the first one I gave
her, I swear," said the little angel. "Plus, she
needed them. Each time she was just about to
give up and cry."

"And now she has given up and she is
crying."

The little angel winced. "I shoved her
toward the trash can that last time. I was

hoping she'd realize that she could roll the trash can over to the bench. Then she could turn it over and climb from the bench to the bottom of the trash can. With that stick she picked up, she could have reached Kathy." He hung his head. "It didn't work. Sorry."

"Hey." The archangel cleared his throat. "Don't feel so bad. That was a good idea, actually. In fact, you get feathers for both shoves."

The Little Angel of Independence looked with surprise and admiration at the two new feathers that sprouted. "Thank you. But Elena's still in trouble."

"She'll find another way, with your help."

"Not if she keeps crying like that." The little angel shook his head. "It's hard to think when you're crying."

"You'll just have to wait till she's ready."

"I hate to wait," said the Little Angel of Independence. "Maybe if I just gave her another tiny shove . . ."

"No. You can't shove her now, while she's

29

running; she'll go flying and scrape up her knees or something."

"Then what can I do?"

"An idea will come," said the archangel.

No Kathy

Elena ran straight to the soccer field. The game had started, all right, and Sam was playing forward. She waved to him.

Sam didn't wave back. He dodged in and out of the other players and kicked the ball hard.

There was no chance that Sam would stop to help her get Kathy. Plus, he'd never believe her if she told him about the shoves.

Elena sat on the sidelines for a while. She braced herself and waited. But no one shoved her. She waited awhile longer. But she couldn't wait too much longer—not with Kathy stuck like that.

Elena got up and started back, preparing her words as she walked. "Don't worry, Kathy. I'll find someone tall—a nice stranger, not a scary one—maybe even a police officer, and I'll get you down. I'll get you down." She went straight to the bush.

Kathy was gone!

Elena looked around. This area of the park was crowded with lilac bushes. But she was sure this very bush was the right one. After all, there was the bench, close under it. And there was the jungle gym, way to the right. This had to be the bush.

She got on her knees and crawled around the base of the bush. But her giraffe wasn't there.

She climbed on the bench and shook the branches as hard as she could. No giraffe fell out.

She tipped over the wire trash can nearest the bush and examined it thoroughly. It was empty now. The trash person had come and gone.

Elena's heart beat wildly. Someone had taken Kathy. Maybe she had even fallen in the trash can and been hauled away. Oh, no. It couldn't be that. Kathy had to be someplace close.

Elena walked over to the sandbox. The little boy and his mother were gone. What if he took Kathy? What if he took Kathy home with him and Elena never saw her again?

Elena kicked her way through the sandbox. Then she plopped down in despair.

Oh! She fell forward and got sand in her mouth. "Who's doing that?" She spit sand and swiped at the air. "Did you take Kathy?" she called out. "You big bully!" She punched and socked and boxed her phantom torturer.

Elena stood up. "Well, I'll show you, wherever you are. I'll find her. I'll find her all right." She would examine every inch of this park.

Angel Talk

The Archangel of Independence folded his arms across his chest. "Do you know anything about the disappearance of Kathy?"

The little angel nodded. "I knocked her out of the bush."

"But, why?" The Archangel of Independence knit his brows. "I told you not to make Kathy fall into Elena's hands. Remember? We already discussed that."

"Oh, I do remember. And that wasn't what I was trying to do. Elena was watching Sam play soccer when I knocked Kathy down, I swear. She wasn't anywhere near."

"So what was on your mind?"

"I don't know exactly. Somehow I had a feeling that it was the right thing to do." The little angel raised his shoulders, then dropped them in defeat. "I made a mess of things."

"Hmm. Do you know where Kathy is?"

"She fell on an old lady who was sitting on the bench."

"You knocked her onto an old lady? Little angel, did you do that on purpose?"

"Well, yes. The lady looked lonely, and I thought she'd be happy at meeting the giraffe."

"But what about Elena? That's her giraffe, and she loves Kathy."

"I know." The little angel pulled at his ear. "I didn't mean to do anything bad. I went back to Elena at the soccer field and I was by her side as she returned to the lilac bush. It was a total surprise to me that the old lady had gone off somewhere. Oh, please, archangel, help me find a way to bring that old lady and Elena together."

"This is your assignment, little angel. I'm only guiding."

The little angel took a deep breath. "Maybe

35

I'll look for that old lady and then shove her toward Elena."

"What?" The Archangel of Independence shook his head vehemently. "That's the worst idea I have ever heard. If you make an old lady fall, she might break a bone."

"Okay. I'll find the old lady and I'll shove Elena toward her."

"No. You can't shove the old lady and you can't shove Elena."

"But that's my way of doing things," said the little angel.

"Look, you've got Elena boxing the air. She thinks there's someone following her around pushing her."

"Well, there is. Me."

"It's scaring her." The archangel slapped his hands together. "You can't shove them, and that's that."

"Well, then, what can I do?"

"You have to figure that out for yourself."

The Big Kids' Slide

Elena scrutinized the girls jumping rope. She followed a father and son playing catch. She watched the children on the swings. No one held Kathy.

She examined the ground everywhere she went. After all, maybe Kathy fell and somehow got blown or kicked someplace else. A dog might have even picked her up and carried her someplace.

But Kathy wasn't on the ground.

Finally Elena went back to the soccer field. Sam was goalie now. Elena felt a little clutch in her stomach for him. Sam hated being goalie. He always felt terrible if the other side scored while he was goalie. Elena shouldn't bother him while he was so worried. She should sit down and wait for the game to end.

"Hey!" A soccer player stumbled and fell against Elena. "Uh, sorry." The boy looked confused. Then he brightened. "You're Sam's sister, aren't you?"

"Yes."

"Watch out." The boy dashed off after the ball.

"Time out!" Sam walked over to Elena. He didn't look happy. "What's the matter?"

"Kathy needs help."

"I told you I'd ask someone to help after the game."

"But she needs help now. Someone kidnapped her."

Sam came closer and lowered his voice. "Whisper, okay? I don't want anyone else to know what a nut you are. What do you mean, someone kidnapped her?"

"She's gone."

Sam put his hands on his hips. "She's not in the bush anymore?"

"No. Someone took her."

"No one would take that nasty giraffe. She just fell. She's probably on the ground somewhere."

"She's not. I looked."

"Look again." Sam turned his back and walked toward the goalposts. He glanced over his shoulder. "And don't bother me. I'll help you when I'm through."

Elena walked back slowly through the park, looking everywhere one more time. No Kathy. She could see the jungle gym now, and the bush beyond it. She could see that the empty top branches swayed in the wind.

She stopped at the little kids' slide and sat on the lowest step of the ladder with her elbows on her knees and her chin in her hands. Walking around the park wasn't doing any good. Kathy wasn't on the ground. She just wasn't.

Elena felt something on her shoulder. It wasn't quick like a shove. It was soft and warm, like an encouraging pat. What a funny sensation. She reached across and rubbed the back of her shoulder.

Where was Kathy? If she wasn't on the ground, maybe she was somewhere higher. Maybe she got blown from one bush to another.

How could Elena see into all the bushes?

She stood up. The jungle gym was pretty high. So was the little kids' slide. But the big kids' slide was even higher. In fact, it was so high that little Kathy was afraid of it. So Elena had never gone down it before.

If Elena went to the top of the big kids' slide, she could see out over most of the park. She might see Kathy that way.

Elena walked slowly toward the slide.

A couple of big boys came running along the path, throwing a basketball back and forth. They left the ball on the ground, scampered up the ladder of the big kids' slide, and zoomed down the slide. Then they went up the ladder again. But this time they waddled down the slide on their feet, knees bent and hands holding on to the sides. They laughed and ran off toward the basketball courts, bouncing the ball between them.

Elena stood at the base of the slide. She held on to the rails of the ladder and looked around. The noise of the boys was far away by now, but she still felt jittery. If they came back while she was trying to climb the ladder, they might rush her so that she got nervous and fell. Or they might try to pass her and knock her off the ladder by accident.

Kathy was right. The big kids' slide was dangerous.

Elena dropped her hands from the rails. Nothing was working out today. Big tears rolled down her cheeks.

Oh. It was raining purple. Elena looked up. Flower petals fell gently on her face. Then the petal-rain stopped, just like that. But her head and shoulders were totally covered with petals. Lilac petals. How strange. It was almost as though the bush were reminding her of how lonely and scared Kathy must be right now.

Elena put her hands back on the ladder rails. She climbed up halfway. Her breath quickened. She looked around. She could see a lot from this height, but she knew she'd see a lot more from the top. She held tight and climbed, stopping after each step to look around.

Angel Talk

I told you not to shove."

"You said not to shove the old lady or Elena. You didn't say not to shove the soccer players."

The Archangel of Independence looked at the little angel critically. "Maybe you should be called the Little Angel of Arguments."

"I'm not trying to argue."

"You're certainly doing a good job of it, anyway." The archangel tapped his finger on the center of the little angel's chest. "No more shoves. And that's final."

"All right," said the Little Angel of Independence.

"And that trick with the lilac petals was questionable, too. It felt like magic to Elena, and magic can be scary, too."

"She didn't box the petals."

The archangel sighed. "You are a difficult one."

"Well, you keep refusing to tell me what to do. So I have no choice but to try whatever I can think of."

The archangel chuckled. "I suppose you're right. Okay. And patting her on the shoulder was really good. That was reassuring. You can experiment. Just no more shoves."

The Heart

"I did it," Elena said to herself, squatting on the top of the slide ladder. "I did it, I did it!" She held on to the rails tight and looked down into the bushes all around.

Then her eyes wandered to the people. Children played here and there. An old lady sat on the bench on the side of the lilac bush, sewing. A mother pushed her baby in a carriage.

There was no sign of Kathy anywhere.

Elena looked carefully at everything again. Then her eyes came back to the old lady. She had on a straw hat with plastic fruit and a pretty flowered dress. Silver flashed from the old lady's lap. And there was something familiar there, too: tan and black. "Hello, lady," she called.

The old woman shaded her eyes with one hand and stretched her neck toward Elena's voice. "Yoo-hoo, on the slide, are you talking to me?"

"I know you." Elena looked down the slide, then she looked down the ladder, then she looked down the slide again. All right, she might as well. She carefully positioned herself, then let her hands go free and slid to the bottom. It was great.

Elena walked over toward the bench. "You're the voting booth lady at King School."

"That's right. I'm Mrs. Carrillo." Mrs. Carrillo smiled. "But you're too young to vote."

"I went with my mother. She said hello to you." Elena stood at a distance and tried to get a better look at what was in the folds of Mrs. Carrillo's skirt. "That's my school."

"Your school. Well, that's wonderful." Mrs. Carrillo finished sewing and cut the thread. Then she cocked her head to one side. "Have you been crying, dear?"

Elena nodded. "I miss my giraffe. I've looked everywhere for her."

"Why, do you know, just this morning a giraffe fell out of the sky and hit me on the head. I went walking around the park, asking children who it belonged to, but no one knew." Mrs. Carrillo held up the giraffe. "Is it yours?"

Elena grabbed the giraffe and pressed it to her cheek. It was Kathy at last. She kissed her forehead right between the horns, where Kathy loved being kissed the most. But then she examined the giraffe carefully. "She's so much like my giraffe. But this one has a shiny silver heart on her tummy."

"Oh, that's your giraffe," Mrs. Carrillo said. "She had a little tear. So I sewed that heart patch on."

"I love her," said Elena. "And I loved her even with a tear."

"Well, I knew that, dear. I could tell she'd been loved hard. She must be very lovable."

"She is," said Elena. "She has a good heart. Deep inside her."

"Of course." Mrs. Carrillo nodded. "Don't you like the patch? If you don't like it, I can take it off again."

Elena slowly outlined the satin heart with her finger. "It's a nice patch," she finally said. "Now everyone can see on the outside what a beautiful heart she really has."

"That's exactly what I was thinking." Mrs. Carrillo smiled and pushed her thick glasses back up the ridge of her nose. "Tell me, what's your giraffe's name?"

"Kathy."

"What a pretty name. And what's yours?"

"Elena."

"It's nice to meet you, Elena. I certainly enjoyed taking care of Kathy."

Elena turned Kathy over in her hands. Then she hugged her tight. "Thank you."

Mrs. Carrillo glowed. "I like sewing. Do you?"

"I don't know how to sew," said Elena.

"It isn't very hard." Mrs. Carrillo opened her sewing basket and pulled out a small ball of brown yarn. "I was just thinking, would Kathy like a new tail?"

Elena peeked into the sewing basket. "You have a ball of red yarn, too."

Mrs. Carrillo took out the red yarn. "Would she rather have a red one?"

"Red's her favorite color."

"And would you like to sew it on yourself?"

"I don't think so," said Elena. "I'll just watch you."

Mrs. Carrillo wrapped the yarn around her hand several times until she had a thick bunch of loops. Then she tied together one end of the loop and cut through the other end. It made a big bushy tail. While Mrs. Carrillo sewed the tail onto Kathy, Elena fumbled through the sewing basket. "You have a peanut butter jar full of buttons."

"Take it out, why don't you?"

52

Elena held up the jar and turned it in her hands. "So many buttons."

Mrs. Carrillo laughed. "I've had a lot of years to collect them."

Elena pointed. "There are two purple-blue matching buttons."

"Those are cornflowers," said Mrs. Carrillo.

"They look like eyes."

"Why, so they do." Mrs. Carrillo leaned over and took a closer look. "Perfect eyes for a giraffe."

Elena picked the buttons out of the jar and hummed as Mrs. Carrillo sewed them on. She saved Kathy's one old eye in her pocket.

Then Mrs. Carrillo handed Kathy back to Elena.

"She's perfect. Now no one will call her beat-up." Elena kissed Kathy and sat down beside Mrs. Carrillo. "I like the park."

"So do I. I come to do my mending." Mrs. Carrillo put her scissors, yarn, thread, and needle back into the sewing basket. "And I listen to the birds. I have a bird named Sweetie Pie. She loves to eat parsley."

"I don't have any pets. Just a brother. He's over there." Elena pointed toward the soccer field.

"A brother! Well, you must be the luckiest girl in the world. I like to listen to brothers and sisters. I sit here and listen to all the children. To tell you the truth, I'd really like to talk with people. But everyone's too busy. So I just listen."

"Too busy to talk?" Elena put Kathy down on the bench and swung her legs. "I love to talk. Ma calls me a chatterbox."

"Well, you just stay a chatterbox always." Mrs. Carrillo smoothed her skirt. "What do you like to do in the park?"

"Just about everything."

"There must be something you like best." Mrs. Carrillo nodded to herself. "Let me guess. I know, I bet you like the slide best.

That's where you were sitting a moment ago."

Elena looked at the slide. "That was the first time I ever went on the big kids' slide." She sat up tall. "Usually I stay on the swings and take care of Kathy while my brother, Sam, goes on that slide. But today you took care of Kathy, and I climbed to the top."

"To the very top!" Mrs. Carrillo clapped her hands and laughed. She took Kathy and held her up to her ear. "Kathy tells me she's very proud of you."

"I can climb the jungle gym, too."

Mrs. Carrillo laughed. "You're quite an acrobat."

"I can do other things, too. Watch." Elena hopped off the bench and did a somersault on the grass.

"Oh, my, that's excellent."

"And I'm working on cartwheels." Elena did a cartwheel on the grass.

"That's coming along very nicely. All you need is to remember to point those toes, and it will be just right." Mrs. Carrillo looked at Kathy. "Why, could it be? I think Kathy just stomped her front hooves. Do you think she'd like to be an acrobat, too?"

Elena laughed and helped Kathy do a cartwheel across Mrs. Carrillo's lap.

Angel Talk

"Did you whisper in Mrs. Carrillo's ear and make her think Kathy was talking?"

"No." The Little Angel of Independence blinked. "I swear I didn't."

"Hmm. And did you make Kathy stomp her hooves?"

"No."

"Hmm." The Archangel of Independence pressed his lips together. "This Mrs. Carrillo has quite an imagination."

"Yes. And she's doing my job."

"How so?"

"She's giving Elena lots of praise, so Elena feels more self-confident and independent. I'm glad of that, of course. But I don't see how I'll earn any more feathers this way." The little angel climbed up a maple tree, swung from a branch, and landed beside the archangel again.

"You're the real acrobat."

The little angel laughed. "I'm just a climber."

"A climber who's earning lots of feathers. With every word of encouragement from Mrs. Carrillo, you earn another one."

"Really? Why?"

"Well, it was your action that brought them together. Somehow you sensed that knocking Kathy out of the tree onto Mrs. Carrillo's head would make things turn out right. You have good instincts. And just look at your wings."

The Little Angel of Independence spread his wings. "They're almost fully feathered."

"And you're not even holding my hand," said the archangel.

The little angel smiled at the Archangel of Independence. "I guess I'm getting ready to do this sort of work on my own."

"I guess you are."

Doughnuts

Elena brushed the grass off her hands and settled herself again on the bench.

"Do you like doughnuts, Elena?"

"Sure. Everyone likes doughnuts."

Mrs. Carrillo took a white paper bag out of her pocket. "I always stop by the doughnut shop on my way to the park. Today I bought jelly. How's that sound?" She handed the bag to Elena.

"There's only one," said Elena.

"That's okay. You eat it. I can buy myself another one on the way home."

"Let's split it," said Elena.

"That's a fine idea. You're such a smart girl."

Elena ripped the doughnut in half. Red jelly squished out onto her hands. She gave half to Mrs. Carrillo and ate the other half.

Then she licked the jelly off her palms and threw the paper bag in the trash can.

Mrs. Carrillo took a pillowcase out of her sewing basket. "I need to mend the hem on this. And, look, the thread on this needle is just about used up. Can you thread a needle?"

"Sure."

Mrs. Carrillo handed Elena the white thread and a needle. "My eyes aren't so sharp anymore. Usually I have to use a magnifying glass to thread my needles. But now you're here. I'm so lucky today."

Elena carefully inserted the tip of the thread into the tiny hole of the needle. There. She handed it to Mrs. Carrillo and watched her sew. It didn't look that hard. "Is there anything else to mend in your basket?"

"Well, I think so." Mrs. Carrillo pulled out another pillowcase. "And here's another needle."

Elena threaded her own needle and worked carefully.

Mrs. Carrillo smiled admiringly. "Such

neat, tight stitches. Why, you're the best helper in the world."

Elena and Mrs. Carrillo sat together, sewing and talking about many things, while Kathy slept between them.

When the church bells began to ring, Elena said, "I have to go meet my brother, Sam, now. Will you be here tomorrow?"

"I'll be here."

"Will you be here every day?"

"As long as the weather's nice."

"Good," said Elena. "Then we can talk."

"And I can take care of Kathy while you do your acrobatics and whatever else you want to do. You're good at so many things."

Elena realized it was true. She had done lots of new things today, and she'd done them well. And Kathy hadn't been part of them. She loved Kathy; she loved her so much. But there wasn't really anything for Kathy to do at the park. "Maybe it'll be just me. Kathy needs to rest at home sometimes."

"Yes, of course." Mrs. Carrillo nodded. "And a big girl like you needs to go out on her own now and then."

Elena nodded back. She held Kathy in one hand and got up to go. She looked hard at Mrs. Carrillo for a moment. Then Elena gave Mrs. Carrillo a quick hug.

The plastic fruit on the old woman's hat danced.

"Tell me," asked Mrs. Carrillo, "what's your favorite kind of doughnut?"

"Glazed."

"Well, then, tomorrow I'll bring two, one for you and one for me. Toodle-loo."

Angel Thoughts

The newest Archangel of Independence flew to the top of the church steeple and stood there, stretching his wings as the music of the church bells faded away. He had always enjoyed church bells, but now they would mean so much more to him because they would remind him of how he had earned his last feathers.

Tomorrow was a big day for Elena: She would come to the park with empty hands, and Kathy would lie safe on Elena's pillow all day. The archangel looked down at his own empty hands. He was alone now—an archangel, in charge of himself. Well, that felt good.

Tomorrow would be a big day for him, too: He'd begin his work guiding little angels. But, for now, he'd fly anywhere he liked. All on his own.

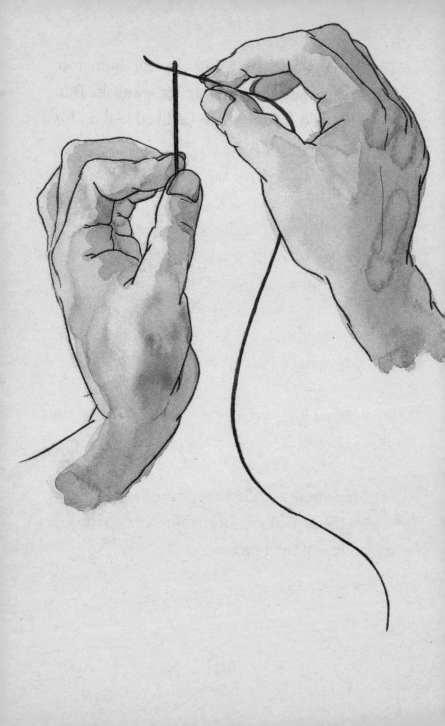

How to thread a needle:

* Choose a thread color that closely matches the fabric you'll be sewing.

* Cut a length of thread (it's usually wise to cut a little more than you think you'll need so that you won't run out too soon).

* Try to cut the thread at an angle—that will make it easier to put through the needle.

* Hold the needle in one hand and the thread in the other, as shown in this drawing.

* The hole is called the "eye" of the needle. Insert the angled end of the thread into the eye at the top of the needle.

Meet the Little Angel of Courage
in the next Aladdin **Angelwings**

№. 4 One Leap Forward

Watch closely now," said the Archangel of Courage.

The Little Angel of Courage watched the girls in their tutus. She looked for anyone who was hesitating or hanging back. But all of them were paying attention to the ballet teacher, and all of them tried every move the teacher demonstrated. "I don't see anyone who needs courage," said the little angel.

The Archangel of Courage smiled knowingly. "Look harder."

A tall girl held her chin high. A short girl held her back straight. A blond girl was sweating, but smiling, too. A redhead had determination written all over her face. The Little Angel of Courage looked hard at each girl. No one looked timid. Instead, they looked cheerful in their blue leotards, like a row of cornflowers on a spring morning.

The girls turned to the barre. They hurried in crisscrossing paths to their spots. The little angel could see that they had fixed spots at the barre: they were arranged according to height. As the third little girl in the line turned, she gave a quick wave.

A boy on the other side of the room jumped to his feet and waved back wildly. Then he sat down on the observation bench and stared, both legs swinging under him, his lips slightly parted.

The girls put one leg on the barre and both arms above their head in an arc.

The boy on the bench reached his arms above his head in an arc, too.

The girls stood with one hand on the barre now and kicked one leg, toe pointed to the side.

The boy stretched his legs out in front of

him on the bench and pointed his toes.

The girls put both hands on the barre and arched backward.

The boy arched backward. Farther and farther. So far, he fell off the bench with a crash.

The class looked at him.

The boy hopped back onto the bench and sat on his hands, not moving. He looked at his knees.

"I understand," said the Little Angel of Courage. "What's his name?"

"Paul. He comes to ballet class every Tuesday afternoon and watches his sister dance. He imitates all her moves." The Archangel of Courage touched the Little Angel of Courage on the cheek. "You need only five more feathers to fill out your wings and you'll be an archangel. I'm sure this job is worth a lot of feathers. Do you think you can help Paul?"

The Little Angel of Courage looked at Paul. Earning her wings, one feather at a time, was hard—but that was the pace she liked. After all, there was something about the whole idea of flying around as an archangel that made her stomach flutter in a sick way. Once she was an archangel, she'd have to guide little angels, and she wasn't sure at all that she knew how to do that.

But she was sure she could help this boy, and if she could help him, well, then, she should. Maybe she could do this job in only four feathers, so then she'd have a little more time before the bell rang announcing that she'd earned her wings—a little more time before she had to face becoming an archangel.

The Swan

Paul put his sneakers back on as he waited for his sister, Silvia, outside the dressing room. Older girls, in purple leotards, were already rushing out onto the wooden dance floor to warm up before the next lesson. Paul pressed against the wall to stay out of their way.

Silvia appeared beside him. "Let's go."

Paul followed her down the stairs of Camilla's School of Dance and out to the sidewalk.

"You fell off the bench today," said Silvia.

Paul already knew that. He walked a little faster.

"What were you doing?"

"Nothing."

Silvia hung her tote from her shoulder so

that her arms were free. She moved her arms in front of her as she walked.

"That's part of ballet, isn't it?" asked Paul. He swung his arms in a circle.

"Yup. These are called 'positions.'" Silvia glided along. Her arms streamed behind her now. Her head tilted forward gracefully.

Paul couldn't believe his eyes. "You're a swan."

"That's a nice thing to say. There's a famous ballet about a swan."

Paul remembered. He'd watched that ballet on TV. He had imagined he was the Prince.

"It's called *Swan Lake*. Someday I'm going to dance in that ballet." Silvia skipped ahead, and now she was his sister again, not a swan at all.

Paul swung his arms in a circle. "Am I the Prince?"

"Huh?" Silvia stopped and looked at Paul as though he were nuts. "What are you talking about?"

Paul felt stupid. Of course Silvia didn't think he was the Prince. Paul didn't know how to do ballet. He only knew how to do ordinary things, like run. He ran in a circle around Silvia, swinging his arms wildly. "These are my fastest sneakers."

"Who cares about speed? You don't have to be fast to do ballet." Silvia sniffed and did a little twirl. Her tote smacked against her knees.

Paul ran ahead of Silvia the rest of the way home.

Don't miss these other
Aladdin *Angelwings* stories:

№ 4

One Leap Forward

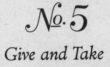

№ 5

Give and Take

№ 6

No Fair

Earn Your Wings!
essay contest

Win

✱ A $250 Gap gift certificate

✱ Your name in an Aladdin Angelwings book

✱ $100 worth of Simon & Schuster
Children's books

✱ $250 worth of Simon & Schuster Children's
books donated to your school's library

✱　　✱　　✱

Describe your good deed in
300 words or less for your
chance to win.

Have you earned your
Angelwings?

Official Rules
Aladdin Angelwings
"Earn Your Wings" Contest

1. No purchase necessary. Submission must include one original essay on the good deed you have done (not to exceed 300 words). Entries should be typed (preferable) or printed legibly. Mail your essay to: Simon & Schuster Children's Publishing Division, Marketing Department, Aladdin Angelwings "Earn Your Wings" Contest, 1230 Avenue of the Americas, New York, New York 10020. Each essay can only be entered once. Contest begins September 15, 1999. Entries must be received by December 31, 1999. Not responsible for postage due, late, lost, stolen, damaged, incomplete, not delivered, mutilated, illegible, or misdirected entries, or for typographical errors in the rules. Entries are void if they are in whole or in part illegible, incomplete, or damaged. Enter as often as you wish, but each entry must be different and mailed separately. Essays will be judged by Simon & Schuster Children's Publishing on the following basis: 80% good deed done, 20% writing ability. All entries must be original and the sole property of the entrant. Entries must not have been previously published or have won any awards. All submissions become the property of Simon & Schuster and will not be returned. By entering, entrants agree to abide by these rules. Void where prohibited by law.

2. Winner will be selected from a judging of all eligible entries received and will be announced on or about March 1, 2000. Selected entrant will be notified by mail.

3. One Consumer Grand Prize: The winner will receive a $250 gift certificate at Gap Clothing Stores, $100 worth of Simon & Schuster Children's Publishing books, have $250 worth of Simon & Schuster Children's Publishing books donated to his or her school's library, and have his or her name appear in a future Aladdin Angelwings book. The winner's essay may appear in future publication(s) from Simon & Schuster or advertising for the Aladdin Angelwings series.

4. Contest is open to legal residents of U.S. and Canada (excluding Quebec). Winner must be 14 years of age or younger as of December 31, 1999. Employees and immediate family members (or those with which they are domiciled) of Simon & Schuster, its parent, subsidiaries, divisions, and related companies and their respective agencies and agents are ineligible. Prize will be awarded to the winner's parent or legal guardian.

5. Prize is not transferable and may not be substituted except by Simon & Schuster. In the event of prize unavailability, a prize of equal or greater value will be awarded.

6. All expenses on receipt of prize, including federal, state, provincial and local taxes, are the sole responsibility of the winner. Winner's legal guardian will be required to execute and return an Affidavit of Eligibility and Release and all other legal documents that Simon & Schuster may require (including but not limited to an assignment to Simon & Schuster of all rights including copyright in and to the winning essay and the exclusive right of Simon & Schuster to publish the winning entry in any form or media) within 15 days of attempted notification or an alternate winner will be selected.

7. By accepting a prize, winner grants to Simon & Schuster the right to use his/her entry and name and likeness for any advertising, promotional, trade, or any other purpose without further compensation or permission, except where prohibited by law.

8. Simon & Schuster shall have no liability for any injury, loss, or damage of any kind, arising out of participation in this contest or the acceptance or use of a prize.

9. The winner's first name and home state or province, available after 3/15/00, may be obtained by sending a separate, stamped, self-addressed envelope to: Winner's List, Aladdin Angelwings "Earn Your Wings" Contest, Simon & Schuster Children's Publishing Marketing Department, 1230 Avenue of the Americas, New York, NY 10020.